Layout Artist : C.A. Penchavez

To order additional copies of this book, contact:
Xlibris Corporation
1-888-795-4274
www.Xlibris.com
Orders@Xlibris.com

# A Garden Tale

Written by Brenda S. Richards
Illustrated by Christine J. Amata

## Dedication

For LPR and SGR, who remind me to see the beauty around us everyday!
BSR

For Pete, Nicholas, Nathan, Alex and Anthony, who make all my days beautiful.
CJA

In each growing garden,
    A wee village stands.
In this one, best friends,
    They walk hand in hand.

Liam Patrick, an elf,
    With a handsome, brave face
Holds the hand of a fairy,
    Miss Sweet Sadie Grace.

They march through the garden,
    Their playground and home.
To visit their neighbors,
    Together they roam.

They call upon Ants,
     The first critters they meet.
And they all sit together
     For a wee bite to eat.

They dine on Blueberries,
    Strawberries and Cream.
Then they all settle in
    For an afternoon dream.

Their nap interrupted!

A Chickadee came
To tell them about
The Summer-time Games.

"Each morning, the garden,

Dampened with Dew,
Comes alive as the sun shines,
Re-freshed and new."

"In this garden," she tells,

"The Earthworms and Frogs,
They love to run races
And jump over logs."

"All Garden friends play,
    The big and the small.
But this year, I fear,
    We can't play at all.

"A Hobgoblin has come
    And ruined our fun.
He scared off my friends
    To the very last one."

"A hobgoblin, you say?"
        Asks the brave elf so clear.
"What's that?" asks the fairy,
        Without any fear.

"He lives in the Ivy
        At the edge of the wood.
He likes to play tricks,
        But I fear they're no good."

The June-Bug, she tells
    Of a trick he has played.

A Katy-did speaks
    Of the trouble he's made,

"He jumped right out of

The Lima bean row,
And frightened us all

To the Mushrooms, you know!"

Liam Patrick decides
It's his job to protect
The garden, the birds,
And every insect.

"Well, this must stop now!

It's our home. Our Nest!
If he wants to stay,
He must pass my test!"

"What can we do?"
        Asks Sweet Sadie Grace,
Dressed in a sweet pea
        And Queen Anne's lace.

"We'll look for this fellow.
        We'll find where he slumbers.

We'll look in the Onions,
        The peas and cucumbers."

Now Liam and Sadie
  Look high and look low,
To find the hobgoblin,
  Their village's foe.

Next to the Pumpkins
  They find him asleep.
Ever so quietly,
  Upon him they creep.

12

They jump out to scare him.

Liam points a sharp Quill.
The hobgoblin cries out,
   His voice loud and shrill,

"What are you doing?
   I was sleeping right here.

Dreaming of Rabbits,
   But you woke me, oh dear!"

Liam Patrick stands tall,
　　Sadie Grace at his side.
He tells the hobgoblin,
　　Who's scared and wide eyed,

"You've played nasty tricks,
　　Scared our friends. Goodness sakes!
You've frightened the chipmunks,

　　The fireflies and Snakes."

The hobgoblin sits down,
	With tears in his eyes.
To Liam and Sadie,
	Heartfelt, he replies,

"Scared them? Not I!
	I was trying to play,

But they hid in the Toadstools,
	And then ran away.

"I know I look different.
	From here I'm not born,
But I heard of your village

	From the young Unicorn."

"It's a beautiful place.
I've looked all around,
At the plants, and the flowers

And the Vines on the ground.

"I'd love to stay, if you please.
    To your friends I'll explain,
I'd love to live near

    The Wind, sun and the rain.

"The woods, yes, they're nice.
    But this garden I love!
And I can still see the trees
    And the sky up above."

EX cited to share this good news,
They do run.
The elf and the fairy,
Their work almost done.

Sadie tells all her friends,
    The short and the tall,
"Hobgoblin is friendly,
    Just different, that's all.

"He means us no harm.
    He'd like to live here,

In the Yams or the 'taters
    Somewhere rather near."

The friends all agree
    Their garden to share.
And make a new friend,
    A hobgoblin, so rare.

In peace they exist now,
    Hobgoblin and more.
The moral of this story
    Stands true to the core;

Though each flower is different,
    Each is perfect, that's true.
The tulips and daisies,

    And Zinnias too!

The Summer-time Games now
    Return every year.
Hobgoblins and insects
    Compete ear to ear.

And so ends the story
    Of this beautiful place.
A thank you to Liam
    And Miss Sweet Sadie Grace.

Now look in this garden,
Up high and down low.

A through Z are the things
That we've gotten to know.